Stones

Three One Act Plays by
Colleen Neuman

Baker's Plays
c/o Samuel French, Inc.
45 West 25th Street
New York, NY 10010
bakersplays.com

CONTENTS

STONE SOUP

CHARACTERS

TRAMP

SISTER 1

SISTER 2

SISTER 3

SISTER 4

SISTER 5

The play is written for a cast of 6. It may be performed by a larger or smaller cast by using more or fewer **SISTERS**.

No roles are gender specific. **SISTERS**, for example, may be played as **BROTHERS**.

(**TRAMP** *stands at center with back to audience.* **TRAMP** *carries a cooking pot. There is a stone wrapped in an elaborate scarf in one of his pockets. Cup, twigs, match and old spoon are also in his pockets.*)

(**SISTERS** *stand on boxes arranged in a semicircle behind* **TRAMP**. *Their backs are to the audience. The order of the sisters, left to right from the audience's viewpoint, is* **SISTER 4**, **SISTER 5**, **SISTER 1**, **SISTER 2** *and* **SISTER 3**.)

(*There is a stone on the ground off to one side. There is a small log just to right of center.*)

TRAMP. (*turns to face audience*) There was a man.

SISTER 1. (*turns to face audience*) There was a woman.

TRAMP. The man was a tramp who tramped the world around. (*begins a tramp around stage, weaving around* **SISTERS** *on boxes*)

SISTER 1. The woman had a sister . . .

SISTER 2. (*turns to face audience*) Who had a sister…

SISTER 3. (*turns to face audience*) Who had a sister…

SISTER 4. (*turns to face audience*) Who had a sister…

SISTER 5. (*turns to face audience*) Who had a sister. And these sisters kept house…

SISTER 1. And in their house they kept…

SISTER 2. Lard.

SISTER 3. Sardines.

SISTER 4. Mackerels by the crate.

SISTER 5. Fish of every temperament and dimension.

SISTER 1. Rye bread soft as pillows.

SISTER 2. Oatmeals.

SISTER 3. Bacons.

SISTER 4. Spices by the pail.

SISTER 5. Rices by the bag.

SISTER 1. Though never adjoining on the cupboard for they fuss.

SISTER 2. Corn, popped and creamed.

SISTER 3. Onions, chopped, flounced and skewered.

SISTER 4. Creams, soured and whipped.

SISTER 5. Cakes, fat and juicy.

SISTER 1. Pickles, barreled and brined.

SISTER 2. Green beans and all their cousins.

SISTER 3. Won tons.

SISTER 4. An avalanche of potatoes.

SISTER 5. Assorted pies.

SISTER 1. These sisters did not want for food. So, to pass the time, they bickered…

(**SISTERS** *become very contentious.*)

SISTER 2. About the state of the world!

SISTER 3. The price of cabbage!

SISTER 4. The best way to wrap a fish!

SISTER 5. The worst way to wrap a fish!

SISTER 1. The capitals of North Dakota!

SISTER 2. Panama hats!

SISTER 3. Starch or no starch!

SISTER 4. The stars in the firmament!

SISTER 5. Licorice!

SISTERS. *(fold arms and turn faces away from each other)* Huh!

SISTER 1. For bickering was their only entertainment and they kept at it.

TRAMP. *(stops at center)* My feet is all tramped out. A rest will freshen them.

SISTERS. *(have turned to look at* **TRAMP** *as he speaks but now turn faces away)* Huh!

SISTER 1. For these sisters didn't like the smell of a stranger.

TRAMP. *(noticing imaginary river at center)* This looks a likely river. *(Sits on log. Sets down cooking pot. Dips fingers in river. Tastes water.)* Ah. Plain as paste. A river meant for the making of stone soup.

SISTERS. *(disgusted)* Stone soup!

TRAMP. Stone soup don't like fussy water. Plain is best.

SISTERS. But stones?

TRAMP. Stones.

SISTERS. In a soup?

TRAMP. In a soup.

SISTERS. *(turn faces away)* Huh!

SISTER 1. For these sisters is purists and not open to possibility.

TRAMP. *(taking scarf from pocket and unwrapping stone with great care and anticipation)* Not just any stones, mind. Not these common stones we trip over here but this…

(holding stone up for SISTERS *to see)*

THIS is a soup stone.

SISTER 1. *(*SISTERS *are unimpressed.)* A stone…

SISTER 2. Is a stone…

SISTER 3. Is a stone…

SISTER 4. Is a stone…

SISTER 5. Is a stone.

TRAMP. *(Getting up and going from one* SISTER *to the next, left to right, giving each a closer look at the stone.* SISTERS *pretend not to look but are a little curious.)* Ah, my children, what a sheltered life you live. For a stone is a stone except when it's not and a soup stone is a rare thing – born on a night of flying stars and smiling moons.

SISTERS. *(Refuse to be impressed. Turn faces away.)* Huh!

SISTER 3. It's an ordinary stone.

TRAMP. *(Reversing direction. Going from one* SISTER *to the next, right to left, giving each another close look at the stone.* SISTERS *are looking a little more this time.)* Ordinary in looks, as most of us are. But, oh, left to bubble in a pot of the plainest water, why, its soup like you've never had in your life. Soup dropped from heaven. Soup fit for kings and gods. Soup to make strong men tremble and weep.

SISTERS. *(Refuse to be impressed. Turn faces away.)* Huh!

TRAMP. *(picks up cooking pot)* First comes the pot, though the pot itself don't matter to the soup. A pot is a pot.

SISTERS. (**SISTERS** *watch* **TRAMP***'s soup preparations with growing interest but turn their faces away on each "Huh.")* Huh!

TRAMP. *(scooping pot into imaginary river)* Then the water. Too much is worse than not enough. Soup ain't no good drowned.

SISTERS. Huh!

TRAMP. *(Sets pot center. Takes twigs out of pocket and arranges around base of pot.)* And now the combustibles. For cold soup ain't soup at all but only the promise of soup. The caliber of the sticks is of no concern. Any stick makes itself handy to the job will do. A stick is a stick.

SISTERS. Huh!

TRAMP. *(takes match from pocket)* And now a match of no importance. A match is a match. *(Pretends to strike match to sticks. With great drama.)* And now, madams, hold your breaths, cross your fingers and…

(With great drama, slowly lowers the stone into pot. **SISTERS** *can't help themselves – they are watching with great interest.* **TRAMP** *listens – great relief.)*

It's begun.

(sits on log)

SISTER 3. *(suspicious)* How long will it take?

TRAMP. *(mopping at face with scarf)* The stone will know. Trust the stone.

SISTER 4. *(suspicious)* What'll it taste like?

TRAMP. *(Putting scarf back in pocket. Rubbing his tired feet.)* Stone soup ain't never the same. It turns on meteor showers, cloud formations, the lift of the sun, the curve of the moon. *(a very fond memory)* Just yesterday I had the finest stone soup of my life. Of course, there was carrot in it. Stone soup don't depend on carrot though I give THAT carrot credit for its contribution. It was a carrot of high character. There's nobody in the world could grow THAT carrot again.

SISTERS. *(insulted)* Huh!

SISTER 5. *(taking a carrot from her apron pocket)* Our carrots is all the carrot anybody'd ever want. *(holding it up with great pride)* Look at the carrotness of the thing!

TRAMP. *(an indifferent glance at carrot)* No offense to you, madam, or to your carrot, but it don't look to be a soup carrot so much as a stew carrot. And stew carrots is known to be of markedly lesser quality.

SISTER 5. It's a soup carrot or I'm a duck! *(getting off box and going to pot)* I'll prove it! *(defiantly drops carrot in pot)*

TRAMP. *(Jumping up. Horrified.)* Oh! You're all of you strangers to stone soup so don't mean to cause a disaster, but you don't never put in carrot without you put in an equally sublime quantity of celery or the soup turns vinegary and fishy and is ruined. Carrot alone is the death of stone soup. *(hovering over pot with great concern)*

SISTERS. Celery?

TRAMP. Though just any celery won't do. Yesterday's soup had the cleverest celery. It could deal cards and dance the polka.

SISTER 2. *(Insulted. Taking celery from apron pocket.)* Our celery shames it. Our celery got degrees! And salutations! *(getting off box and going to pot)* And traveled to Europe once! *(defiantly drops celery in pot)*

TRAMP. *(Listening to soup. Very concerned.)* It still leans to carrot.

*(***SISTER 2** *puts in more celery. More listening. Still worried.)*

Now it leans to celery!

*(***SISTER 5** *drops in more carrot. A final listen. Great relief.)*

The soup is saved.

SISTERS. Huh!

TRAMP. *(As ***SISTERS 2** *and* **5** *turn to return to boxes. Weeping.)* You put me in mind of my mother.

(SISTERS 2 and 5 stop. All the SISTERS begin to cry as TRAMP tells his sad story.)

TRAMP. Oh my poor mother! On her deathbed, one foot in heaven and one still stuck here in this world with us and all our pulcritudes, she turns to me and says: Child, don't ever eat stone soup without potato or your poor mother's soul will know no peace.

(an especially loud burst of weeping)

This soup hasn't a scrap of potato so must be destroyed to preserve my poor mother's sainted peace.

SISTERS. *(weeping)* We had a mother once ourselves.

SISTER 3. And we got an avalanche of potatoes. *(gets off box and goes to pot)*

TRAMP. I can hear my old mother's voice saying: Twelve for eating…

SISTER 3. *(taking potatoes from apron pocket and dropping them into pot)* One, two, three, four, five, six, seven, eight, nine, ten, eleven, twelve. *(turning to go)*

TRAMP. And one for luck.

(SISTER 3 stops and drops in a final potato. TRAMP listens to soup.)

Peace at last.

(SISTERS 2, 3 and 5 turn to return to boxes.)

Now don't ask me to put in a chicken.

(SISTERS 2, 3 and 5 stop.)

The stone only allows chicken every fourth Tuesday. No exceptions.

SISTER 4. This is!

TRAMP. What is?

SISTER 4. The fourth Tuesday!

TRAMP. Never!

SISTER 4. Count it out! Just last month we had a first Tuesday…

SISTER 5. And then another…

SISTER 2. And then another…

SISTER 3. And here's the fourth Tuesday!

TRAMP. Well, I won't argue you out of it. Numbers is numbers.

SISTER 4. *(pulling a chicken from her apron pocket and holding it high)* Chicken! *(getting off box and going to pot)*

TRAMP. That's a pretty thing. That'll fatten it up.

SISTER 4. *(Holding chicken over pot. To chicken.)* Goodbye Elsabeth. Thanks for all the eggs. *(drops chicken in pot)*

SISTERS. *(hands over hearts and looking to heaven)* To Elsabeth.

*(**SISTERS 2, 3, 4** and **5** turn to return to boxes.)*

TRAMP. But no sausages!

*(**SISTERS 2, 3, 4** and **5** stop.)*

I mean it now! Sausages mustn't be added but between noon and midnight OR between midnight and noon, whichever comes first. The stone remains inflexible about the sausages.

SISTER 1. *(pulling string of sausages from apron pocket)* It's half-past two! *(getting off box and going to pot)*

TRAMP. So soon?

SISTER 1. It happens everyday at just this time.

TRAMP. Well, time flies and we must fly with it.

SISTER 1. *(holds sausages over pot)* There goes as fine a pig as ever lived. Played the trombone and sang ballads. *(drops sausages in pot)*

SISTERS. *(hands over hearts and eyes to heaven)* To the pig.

*(**SISTERS** turn to leave.)*

TRAMP. And don't give a thought to the salt.

*(**SISTERS** stop.)*

Salt is lucky in a soup but we'll just cross fingers and hope for rain.

*(**SISTERS** shrug and turn to leave.)*

(ominously) Still.

*(**SISTERS** stop.)*

TRAMP. Last time I was in a place had saltless stone soup? Next day a mountain slid down on top of that place. Flattened it into next week. Still. It was a SMALL mountain.

SISTERS. *(frightened)* Salt! *(take salt shakers from apron pockets)*

TRAMP. A twinkling.

(**SISTERS** *shake one shake of salt into pot.*)

Or two.

(**SISTERS** *shake two shakes of salt into pot.* **SISTERS** *turn to go.*)

And…

(**SISTERS** *stop.*)

Salt does better with a dose of tarragon. Tarragon soothes the salt.

SISTER 5. *(takes tarragon from apron pocket)* Tarragon!

TRAMP. Just a whisper.

(**SISTER 5** *shakes in one shake.*)

And a half.

(**SISTER 5** *shakes in a little shake.* **TRAMP** *listens to soup.*)

The salt is soothed.

(**SISTERS** *turn to go.*)

Though…

(**SISTERS** *stop.*)

Tarragon raises the whole unfortunate tomato question. And it is a question, madams, that must be answered. The soup depends on it.

SISTERS. Tomato?

TRAMP. Tarragon never leaves the house without a tomato. Why, tarragon without tomato is up without down, it's in without out. It goes against the universe. The soup will be looking for tomato.

SISTER 1. *(taking tomato from apron pocket)* Tomato!

TRAMP. Tuck it in.

> (**SISTER 1** *drops in tomato.* **SISTERS** *turn to go. With tender feeling.*)

Which lands us at spinach.

SISTERS. (**SISTERS** *stop. With tender feeling.*) Spinach?

TRAMP. The orphan of vegetables. Alone and unloved by all but stone soup. The stone soup must have spinach or its heart will break. That's right. Stone soup does have a heart and it does break. It's what sets stone soup apart from the harder world of soups.

SISTER 2. (*taking spinach from apron pocket*) Spinach!

> (*Into the pot.* **SISTERS** *turn to go.*)

TRAMP. And…

> (**SISTERS** *stop.*)

The benediction must follow the spinach, as the night the day. It is ever so.

> (**SISTERS** *and* **TRAMP** *bow heads and fold hands.*)

Bless this soup, onion and all.

SISTERS. Onion?

SISTER 1. Not an onion in it.

TRAMP. (*very upset*) No onion? You can't mean it! I was so sure about the onion! Let me look… (*looking in soup*) Not an onion in sight. And here the benediction is over and done and said "onions" so we can't eat the soup. Why, we'd be eating onionless soup and that'd go against the benediction. Why, it would make a lie of the benediction!

SISTER 3. (*holding up onion*) Onion!

TRAMP. Tumble it in. (*She does. Listens to the soup. Very pleased.*) The benediction is saved.

SISTERS. (*very relieved*) Ah.

> (*turn to go*)

TRAMP. (*with great urgency*) But now, madams, now we're in the home stretch!

(*SISTERS* *stop.*)

TRAMP. Parsnip!

SISTER 4. (*taking parsnip from pockets*) Parsnip! (*into the pot*)

TRAMP. May the soup gods remember your name! Beet!

SISTER 5. (*taking beet from pocket*) Beet! (*about to throw it in pot*)

TRAMP. With a care, madam, for you mustn't bruise the soup.

SISTERS. (*whispering*) Beet! (**SISTER 5** *gently drop beet in pot.*)

TRAMP. Cabbage!

SISTERS. (*with distaste*) Cabbage?

TRAMP. Without cabbage, soup is a bell that don't get rung!

SISTER 1. (*take cabbage from pocket*) Cabbage! (*into the pot*)

TRAMP. We're in the thick of it now, madams! Leek!

SISTER 2. (*take leek from pocket*) Leek! (*into the pot*)

TRAMP. Press on, madams, press on! Zucchini!

SISTER 3. (*take zucchini from pocket*) Zucchini! (*into the pot*)

TRAMP. Courage, madams, courage! Turnip!

SISTER 4. (*take turnip from pocket*) Turnip! (*tnto the pot*)

TRAMP. (*listening to soup*) The soup must catch its breath. (*suddenly weary*) And so will we. (**TRAMP** *sits on log.*)

SISTERS. (*Returning to boxes. Sit down on boxes with relief.*) Ah. (*slumped a bit with weariness*)

TRAMP. Which puts me in mind of the time I had stone soup with the mayor.

SISTERS. (*sit straight up in their excitement*) The mayor?

TRAMP. Oh yes. The mayor has a deep feeling for stone soup. And Mrs. Mayor got out the lace tablecloth. Now I don't expect to be so fancy here with you. I don't mind things ordinary.

SISTERS. (*insulted*) Ordinary!

SISTER 1. (*going to **TRAMP** and pulling lace tablecloth from apron*) We got lace tablecloths will curl your hair!

TRAMP. (*Examining a corner of the tablecloth. Impressed.*) Ah. That brings us up in the world.

(**SISTER 1** *gestures other* **SISTERS** *to join her in pushing boxes together to make a long table behind pot.* **SISTERS** *then arrange tablecloth over it.*)

Puts me in mind of the day I had stone soup with the governor.

SISTERS. *(Stop working for a moment. Impressed.)* The governor!

TRAMP. Oh yes. The governor eats stone soup on all the high holidays. Mrs. Governor got out the china bowls painted to cherry blossoms and the silver spoons embossed with a hummingbird's wing. But crusty bowls and bent spoons don't insult me. I don't mind being common.

SISTERS. *(insulted)* Common!

SISTER 2. *(taking five china bowls from apron pocket)* We got china bowls know to curtsey!

SISTER 3. *(taking five silver spoons from apron pocket)* And our silver spoons do toe–dancing!

TRAMP. *(impressed)* Ah. Now we're a party.

(**SISTERS** *arranging bowls and spoons on table.*)

And that puts me in mind of being at the castle…

SISTERS. *(Stop work for a moment. Impressed.)* The castle!

TRAMP. With the king…

SISTERS. *(more impressed)* The king!

TRAMP. And his queen.

SISTERS. *(hushed reverence)* The queen.

TRAMP. Along with all their little kinglings and queenlings. How the flowers and candelabras did festoon! The stone soup sparkle!

SISTER 4. *(taking a vase with a bouquet of roses from apron pocket)* Our roses will put meat on your bones!

SISTER 5. *(taking a candelabra with candles from apron pocket)* And our candelabra reads Russian literature and goes to the opera on purpose!

TRAMP. *(impressed)* The refinement of it swims my head.

(**SISTERS** *arrange vase and candelabra on table.*)

TRAMP. And Her Highness enthralled in diamonds, His Highness in the purplest purple velvets.

SISTER 1. (**SISTERS** *take pretty hats from apron pockets.*) Our Sunday hats apologize to no man, woman or child.

(**SISTERS** *put on hats.*)

TRAMP. *(impressed)* Paris weeps. *(Suddenly on alert. Quickly goes to soup and listens. Concerned.)* Huh?

SISTERS. Huh?

TRAMP. *(understands)* Oh.

SISTERS. Oh?

TRAMP. *(pleased)* Ah.

SISTERS. Ah?

TRAMP. *(whispering)* The stone whispers: It's done!

SISTERS. *(whispering)* Done!

(**SISTERS** *kneel on floor behind table in the same order in which they stood on their boxes.* **TRAMP** *carries pot with him and uses his cup to ceremoniously serve the soup. Pours soup into first bowl.*)

SISTERS. *(with great anticipation)* Mmmmm.

(**TRAMP** *pours soup into second bowl.*)

Mmmmm.

(**TRAMP** *pours soup into third bowl.*)

Mmmmm.

(**TRAMP** *pours soup into fourth bowl.*)

Mmmmm.

(**TRAMP** *pours soup into fifth bowl.*)

Mmmmm.

(**TRAMP** *scoops his cup full of soup. Sets down pot. Takes spoon from pocket.*)

TRAMP. *(raises spoon in toast)* To the stone!

SISTERS. *(raise their spoons in toast)* To the stone!

TRAMP. *(in hungry anticipation)* To the soup!

SISTERS. *(in hungry anticipation)* To the soup!

(**TRAMP** *and* **SISTERS** *all take one bite in unison. Ecstasy.)*

SISTER 1. Ah. The truest soup of my life.

SISTER 2. A soup both splendid and fragile.

SISTER 3. A truly supernatural soup.

SISTER 4. A soup stands up and gives a speech every New Year's Eve.

SISTER 5. A soup lights up the room.

TRAMP. Lovely.

TRAMP & **SISTERS.** (**TRAMP** *and* **SISTERS** *eat soup in unison. Drink last drops from bowls and cup. Set down bowls and cup with great satisfaction.)* Ah.

TRAMP. Time to tramp on. *(hears something as he picks up pot)* What's that? *(Takes stone out of pot. Listens to it. Astounded.)* Why, the stone means to stay.

SISTERS. *(astounded)* Stay?

TRAMP. *(listens to stone)* Says it never met such stone soup souls as yourselves.

SISTERS. *(surprised)* Us?

TRAMP. *(listens to stone)* Suspects you been stone souping all your lives.

SISTERS. *(more surprised)* All our lives?

TRAMP. *(listens to stone)* In your sleep.

SISTERS. *(pleased)* In our sleep!

TRAMP. *(listens to stone)* With one hand tied behind your back.

SISTERS. *(more pleased)* Behind our back!

TRAMP. *(To the stone. Very emotional.)* Farewell, old friend.

(Holding stone to his heart. To the **SISTERS** *who nod with great feeling after each request.)*

I ask only that you don't wear it out. Use it once or twice a week with plenty of rest in between. Dust it off every Tuesday. And let it sit in the sun on those days the world is kissed with sun.

(A final emotional moment with stone. Hands stone to **SISTER** 1 *who receives it with great reverence and continues holding it with great reverence to end of play. To audience.)*

TRAMP. *(to audience)* And the tramp tramped off.

(Tramps off. As **SISTERS** *are continuing their lines,* **TRAMP** *notices a stone on the ground off to the side. Picks it up, looks it over and decides it will do nicely. Making sure* **SISTERS** *don't see, he wraps it up in his scarf and puts it in his pocket. Continues on his tramp around the stage.)*

SISTER 1. *(stands)* Leaving them there with the stone.

SISTER 2. *(stands)* Which they treasured.

SISTER 3. *(stands)* Dusting it.

SISTER 4. *(stands)* Resting it.

SISTER 5. *(stands)* Sunning it.

SISTER 1. *(steps on to table)* And they never went back to their bickering ways.

SISTER 2. *(steps on to table)* For they never gave a toss about North Dakota...

SISTER 3. *(steps on to table)* Or Panama hats...

SISTER 4. *(steps on to table)* Or any of the rest...

SISTER 5. *(steps on to table)* But only wanted diversion.

SISTERS. Which the stone provided.

SISTER 1. And on stone soup days, all is heaven.

SISTER 2. The sisters going so far as to drag strangers off the road, that those strangers should be fed stone soup.

SISTER 3. Creating a shortage of strangers in the world.

SISTER 4. And there is always the lace.

SISTER 5. And always the china bowls.

SISTER 1. And always the silver spoons.

SISTER 2. And always the Sunday hats which change and improve with the seasons.

SISTER 3. For stone soup deserves the full ride.

SISTER 4. All this...

SISTER 5. From the simple miracle...

(**TRAMP** *is now standing in front of* **SISTER 1.**)

ALL. Of stone soup.

(*bow*)

COSTUMES

TRAMP - Very worn shirt, jacket, trousers, tie and hat.

SISTERS - Housewife dresses with petticoats, patterned
stockings, colorful shoes, matching aprons with roomy
pockets, pretty Sunday hats.

SET

5 sturdy crates or boxes that are all the same size
1 small log

PROPS

cooking pot

twigs

match

old cup

old spoon

2 stones

large elaborate scarf

rubber chicken

string of fake sausages

5 salt shakers

1 tarragon shaker

lace tablecloth

5 china bowls

5 silver spoons

vase of roses

candelabra with candles

fake vegetables – carrots, celery, potatoes, tomato, spinach,
onion, parsnip, beet, cabbage, leek, zucchini, turnip

ROBBERS ARE EVERYWHERE

23

CHARACTERS

MAN
SERVANT
MISSUS
FISH SELLER
BOTTLE SELLER
FLOWER SELLER
RICE SELLER
MOUSE SELLER

The play is written for a cast of 8. It may be performed by a larger cast by adding **SELLERS**.

No roles are gender specific. **MISSUS**, for example, may be played as **MISTER**.

*(Five stools arranged randomly at right. **MISSUS** is seated on elaborate chair left. **SERVANT** stands at her side.)*

MAN. *(Enters right carrying small cloth bag. Takes three coins out of bag and counts them.)* One, two, three gold coins and all mine and all I have in the wide world. *(puts coins back in bag, continues to center and knocks on imaginary door)*

SERVANT. *(Goes to door and opens it. Rude.)* What?

MAN. *(very humble)* I ask to see the Missus who lives in the extravagance of this house.

SERVANT. Missus is rich so don't see rags. Be gone and quick about it. *(closing door)*

MAN. *(before door closes)* Why, I'm a little rich myself.

SERVANT. *(doesn't close door)* Are you?

MAN. I am. *(shakes bag so coins rattle a little)*

SERVANT. *(suddenly polite)* Missus may have a moment.

*(returns to **MISSUS**)*

Missus, a rag at your door.

MISSUS. *(arrogant)* I am rich so don't see rags.

SERVANT. *(crafty)* Rag says he's a little rich.

MISSUS. *(craftier)* Only a little? Well, it's a dull day. Reel him in.

SERVANT. *(Returning to **MAN**. Extremely warm and welcoming.)* Missus will see you.

MAN. *(Goes to **MISSUS**. A humble bow.)* I am honored.

MISSUS. *(Rises. Bows back. Exaggerated politeness.)* The honor is mine. May I be of some service to you?

MAN. Yes, Missus. I live here in the safeness of the town, but now must leave it. For my father lies old and ill at the end of a long road.

MISSUS. *(so sympathetic)* Does he?

MAN. He does. And him longing to see his only son, that being me, and me longing to see him and my heart breaking for his oldness and his illness.

MISSUS. And mine breaking along with yours.

MAN. Ah, it's good of you. But here's the pinch.

(Holding out bag. MISSUS itches to get her hands on it but controls herself.)

In this bag is my fortune of three coins and all I own in the universe. But to see my old dad I got to go out on the dark and dangerous road where robbers are everywhere.

MISSUS. *(shocked)* Are they?

MAN. Oh yes, Missus. And those robbers, they'd see me coming and knock me over the head with a stick and get their dirty robbers' hands on my coins and that's the last I'd see of them. And that's the pickle.

MISSUS. It is. For to see the one, that being your dad, you got to risk the other, that being your coins.

MAN. My eyes don't close for worry of it. And as I'm a child in these matters, my three coins being the only coins ever I had, and here you are rich with millions of the things, I come to ask: How am I to go down that dark and dangerous road to see my old dad and keep my coins safe all at one and the same time?

MISSUS. There's one way only out of the soup. Your bag and your coins in it got to stay here in my house and under my thumb, as safe from the local robber population as my own.

MAN. I'd never ask it!

MISSUS. No need. I offer. *(wanders away a step or two, feigning indifference)* It's yours to do or no, which if you don't there's no help for you and your coins'll be swallowed up by villains.

MAN. *(can't hand bag over fast enough)* Here they are!

MISSUS. *(holding bag close)* And here they'll stay, as if my own.

MAN. (**SERVANT** *escorts him out quickly.*) And now I'm off on that dark and dangerous road with my old dad wasting away at the end of it.

MISSUS. May you find him mended and up and dancing.

MAN. A happy hope!

*(Hardly has time to bow as **SERVANT** pushes him out the door. **MAN** exits right as **MISSUS** and **SERVANT** burst out laughing.)*

MISSUS. *(relishing the joke)* Robbers are everywhere! *(Sits. Opens bag and shakes out coins.)* Three coins, a piffling three. *(not impressed)* And the whole three of them small and tired and thin.

SERVANT. And all three dented.

MISSUS. *(with growing enthusiasm)* Ah, but they're gold, real gold.

SERVANT. And all three yours.

MISSUS. And me doing not a thing to grease the getting but letting a poor man make his own mistake. Which is how poor men stay so poor and at the bottom of the world. *(handing bag and coins to **SERVANT**)* Bag them up, haul to vault and stuff them in.

SERVANT. Yes, Missus.

(exits left)

MAN. *(Enters right. Tired and dusty.)* Time goes by. You can't stop it. And even dark and dangerous roads come to an end at last.

(knocks on door)

SERVANT. *(He has returned without bag of coins and resumed post next to chair. Now goes to door and opens it. Rude.)* What?

MAN. *(expecting a warm welcome)* I am returned.

SERVANT. *(trying to close door)* Missus is rich so don't see rags.

MAN. *(stops door from closing)* Oh, but look again and see who it is, so dusty from the road and thin from the work of walking it that you don't know me. It is my coins Missus keeps that I come now to collect.

SERVANT. *(Recognizes* MAN. *Trying harder to close door.)* Be gone and quick about it!

MAN. *(struggling to stop door from closing)* My coins first, if it's no trouble...

SERVANT. It's all trouble! *(slams door)*

MAN. *(Calls through closed door. Perfectly willing to wait.)* I'll wait then. Till it's no trouble at all. *(sits down outside door)*

SERVANT. *(Goes to* MISSUS. *Alarmed.)* Missus, a rag at your door!

MISSUS. *(the usual arrogance)* I am rich so do not see rags.

SERVANT. Not just any rag but that rag owns that bag of three coins lately pounced upon by us!

MISSUS. *(annoyed)* Send him away.

SERVANT. I sent and sent but he won't be sent and is out there waiting!

MISSUS. For?

SERVANT. Us to go out or him to get let in, either one, so he canst grub back his coins!

MISSUS. *(very sure of herself)* His thin and tired and dented three coins are secreted in amongst my mountains of coins for good and for keeps. He'll give up. They always do. *(Gets up. Thinking it over.)* Though while we don't open the door to him we can't open it to ourselves cause of him being out there waiting.

SERVANT. *(resigned)* We got to outwait the waiting.

MISSUS. *(indignant)* It don't matter for you but I'm rich and not to be inconvenienced! So he's to be got rid of. *(She's going to enjoy this. Very crafty and scheming.)* And here's how we hatch it. *(She pulls out a small cloth bag identical to the small cloth bag with the coins.)* Do you see how this is a twin to the bag containing the rag's coins?

SERVANT. *(takes a close look)* Why, it's a miracle of sameness, top to bottom.

MISSUS. These bags are common conveyances in the district so we all got them. Take it.

SERVANT. *(takes it)* Yes, Missus.

MISSUS. Let the weasel in and keep the bag back of you. And when's he's in, hop to it out to my garden. *(gesturing left)* Look in garden till you got three stones, all three small and thin and with the shape of a coin to them. *(even more cunning and scheming)* Slip them in bag. Tie them in tight. And wait for the word from me.

(sits)

SERVANT. Yes, Missus.

(He is nervous about all this but goes to door, holding bag behind back. Opens door. Gestures **MAN** *in.)*

Missus will see you.

(exits left, being careful **MAN** *doesn't see bag behind his back)*

MAN. *(Goes to* **MISSUS.** *Bows. Still expecting a warm welcome.)* I am returned, Missus.

MISSUS. *(icy)* Are you?

MAN. I am. The road was long but at the end of it I found my old dad, who's not so ailing as once he was cause of how my visit cheered him up.

MISSUS. *(icier)* And what is that to me?

MAN. *(put in his place)* Why, not a thing, Missus, and I only come to collect my bag of coins.

MISSUS. My servant's gone to get them…

*(***SERVANT*** hurries on left with bag.)*

And here he is and there they are…

*(***SERVANT*** hands bag to* **MAN.***)*

And off you go.

*(***SERVANT*** rushes* **MAN** *out.)*

MAN. Ah, my precious coins at last… *(opening bag despite being rushed out)* Stones? *(Stops.)* This bag is a bag of stones.

(Going back to **MISSUS.** *Handing her the bag. Still not suspicious.)*

So here it is back, as it's yours and not mine and a mistake's been made.

MISSUS. *(not taking the bag)* Rich women do not make mistakes which is how we stay so round and rich.

MAN. *(starting to panic)* But I must have my bag and my three coins in it.

MISSUS. *(getting up)* You rattle on about these coins but, now I think of it, I never saw any such coins. I never opened your bag for rich women got fine manners and don't snoop.

*(advancing on **MAN** as **MAN** backs up)*

Ah, I'm seeing it now. Why, there was not a thing but stones in that bag at the start! You spun a crooked scheme to rob me of three of my coins! Is that how you make your crooked living? Come asking advice and then contriving whatsoever coins you can into your ratty bag!?

MAN. *(horrified)* No, Missus! The only coins I look for are my own back!

MISSUS. *(very tragic)* I trusted you and graspy double dealings are my reward for it!

MAN. Nothing like it! You're right to trust me!

MISSUS. Do you trust me?

MAN. Oh yes, Missus!

MISSUS. *(Grasps **MAN**'s hand that holds the bag. Gives it a hard shake.)* Then there's your reward for it! Take it and run or I'll engage the police and you'd look good locked up.

*(**SERVANT** bounces **MAN** out the door. **MISSUS** and **SERVANT** burst into laughter.)*

MAN. *(He stands outside the door, dumbfounded at his loss. Laughter continues.)* Stones. Cold, empty stones…

(Looks at the closed door and hears the laughing behind it. The light goes on.)

Robbers ARE everywhere. And them robbers in that house didn't hit me over the head with a stick but with a lie and so robbed my coins from me. Up to her chins in coins and still dirties her hands snatching my few. That's the rot of greed.

(**MISSUS** *and* **SERVANT**, *still laughing, exit left.*)

And as greed took them, it's greed'll get them back.

(*slides stones back into bag*)

And me to market to scare up a crowd.

(*going right as* **SELLERS** *enter right selling their wares, each one going to a stool and setting up shop*)

FISH SELLER. (*with basket of fish*) Mackerel! Herring! Kippers and kale!

BOTTLE SELLER. (*with basket of bottles*) Cider and ale!

FLOWER SELLER. (*with basket of flowers*) Posies and rosies! Pink, purple, red!

RICE SELLER. (*with basket of rice*) Sticky white rice!

MOUSE SELLER. (*with cages of mice*) Pretty white mice!

MAN. (*to* **BOTTLE SELLER**, *feigning great happiness.*) Ah, today was the day of my life!

BOTTLE SELLER. (*Polishing a bottle. Not that interested.*) Was it?

MAN. It was. For a woman rich as cake give me this bag and what's in it. (*pointedly*) As reward.

BOTTLE SELLER. (*immediate interest*) For?

MAN. For trusting her! Though I don't look for reward for such things and do it free.

BOTTLE SELLER. The rich aren't like us.

MAN. That's what I'm learning. I fought to leave it but lost. The rich will win.

BOTTLE SELLER. That they will. (*can't wait to hear*) And reward is?

MAN. (*couldn't be happier about it*) Stones!

BOTTLE SELLER. (*not impressed*) Stones?

MAN. (*couldn't be happier about it all over again*) Stones!

(*wanders a few steps away, beaming.*)

BOTTLE SELLER. (*Takes the bait. Going to* **MOUSE SELLER**. *Points to* **MAN**.) See him there?

MOUSE SELLER. *(a disinterested glance at* **MAN***)* I do.

BOTTLE SELLER. Wish you were him for he's been made rich.

MOUSE SELLER. *(Another quick glance at* **MAN***. Not believing it.)* The man's a rag same as us.

BOTTLE SELLER. But hear it all. A woman rich as cream give him the bag and what's in it as reward. See how he clings to it, desperate and full of wonder.

MOUSE SELLER. *(starting to believe him)* Ah. As reward. That's the way to get rich, if there is one. *(can't wait to hear)* And reward is?

BOTTLE SELLER. *(imagining the possibilities)* Stones!

MOUSE SELLER. *(not impressed)* Stones?

BOTTLE SELLER. Ah, but stones from the rich means diamonds. The rich toss diamonds around like sand. Plus, they get sick of them. They clean out the attic of the old ones and go out and get all new. So he got a bag stuffed with last year's diamonds.

FISH SELLER. *(overhears and joins them)* Who does?

MOUSE SELLER. Him over there. *(imagining the possibilities)* Or rubies!

FISH SELLER. *(Stunned. So loud all the others hear.)* Rubies!

FLOWER SELLER. *(hurrying over)* Where?

FISH SELLER. *(pointing to* **MAN***)* There!

RICE SELLER. *(hurrying over)* Who?

FISH SELLER. *(pointing to* **MAN** *again)* Him!

RICE SELLER. How?

(They crowd around **BOTTLE SELLER** *who tells the story with much whispering and gesturing and pointing.)*

MISSUS. *(Enters left with* **SERVANT***.* **SERVANT** *helps her on with flashy jewelry.)* Off to market to buy a fat fish. And I mean to make a promenade of it, so need elegant protuberances here and there for the rags to eye and envy. For what good is it being rich if there's nobody to wish it was them?

SERVANT. No good at all, Missus.

MISSUS. Lift my golden skirts that they do not touch the common dirt.

SERVANT. Yes, Missus.

(picks up back of cape and walks behind **MISSUS** *as they make a great show of walking to market where* **MAN** *is careful not to be noticed and* **SELLERS** *are arguing)*

RICE SELLER. And I say emeralds!

BOTTLE SELLER. Rich folks don't give a fig for emeralds!

MOUSE SELLER. Not when they can get their fat fingers on rubies!

FLOWER SELLER. Rubies is cheap red glass next to pearls!

BOTTLE SELLER. Diamonds!

RICE SELLER. Emeralds!

MOUSE SELLER. Rubies!

FLOWER SELLER. Pearls!

SERVANT. *(taps* **FISH SELLER** *on shoulder)* Missus looks to buy a fat fish.

FISH SELLER. *(goes to* **MISSUS** *as other* **SELLERS** *continue their debate)* Ah, Missus, I got a fat fish made me think of you soon as I saw it. *(displaying fish)*

MISSUS. Fresh?

FISH SELLER. Took the hook not an hour past.

MISSUS. Wrap it.

*(***FISH SELLER** *pulls out piece of cloth to wrap fish.* **MISSUS** *notices other* **SELLERS** *whispering and talking.)*

What's the news?

FISH SELLER. *(as she wraps)* It's him over there ought to be married, as there's a shortage of rich husbands in the neighborhood.

MISSUS. I'm not married myself and don't mind a husband if he's rich.

FISH SELLER. There he is, ripe for hooking. *(pointing to* **MAN***)*

MISSUS. *(Turns and looks at* MAN. *Aghast.)* Him?!

FISH SELLER. Wrapped in rags and up to his ears in jewels!

BOTTLE SELLER. *(Joining them. Eager to share the story.)* And all from a woman rich as walnuts as reward for him trusting her. Which is a blindness of the rich - that common decency got to be bought and sold.

MISSUS. Bah!

BOTTLE SELLER. *(insulted)* Bah, is it? *(to other* SELLERS*)* Her ladyship says 'bah' to our miracle standing over there.

(Other SELLERS *join them, happy to confirm the story.)*

RICE SELLER. Ah, Missus, it's true as toast.

FLOWER SELLER. Why, the bag's stuffed and rattling like marbles!

BOTTLE SELLER. Diamonds the size of teeth!

FLOWER SELLER. Pearls the size of onions!

RICE SELLER. Emeralds the size of puppies!

MOUSE SELLER. Rubies the size of city rats!

BOTTLE SELLER. *(to* MISSUS*)* So you may take your 'bah' and be blessed with it!

*(*SELLERS, *disgusted with* MISSUS, *return to their stools and go back to work.)*

MISSUS. *(To* SERVANT. *Furious.)* What did you put in that bag?!

SERVANT. *(astounded by it all)* Stones! Three of them! And all three thin and flat with the shape of a coin to them…

MISSUS. *(forcing* SERVANT *to look over at* MAN*)* Look at him over there! Is that him we cheated out of his coins?

SERVANT. It is…

MISSUS. And is that the bag we made use of in the cheat-ing?

SERVANT. It is…

MISSUS. And that same bag rattling with jewels! Every mouth in the market shouts it! And the only place those jewels are from is my house where he's lately been! I stand here robbed!

SERVANT. *(can't believe what he's hearing)* Missus, you're seeing things…

MISSUS. *(warming to her subject)* Ah, I am. And what I'm seeing is his real business was spying, looking in this window and that, eyeing out where I keep my jewels. And when we weren't looking, saw his chance and snuck in and filled his pockets and snuck out. It was me suspected him, didn't I, saying he was up to a crooked scheme!

SERVANT. But you saying that was part of your own crooked scheme.

MISSUS. And that's where I tripped, keeping all my eyes on my crime and no eyes left for his.

SERVANT. But the man was mad to have back his own bag and three coins!

MISSUS. That ratty bag and them piffling coins was all decoy. And my jewels already in his pockets! Fistfuls of them! And when he's safe out the door he slides them in the bag for easy transport and comes here to brag on his boggy friends and make himself out big! *(grudging admiration)* Ah, a genius of thievery.

SERVANT. Missus, you're mixed in your head, I think…

MISSUS. *(instantly suspicious)* There's plenty in my head and here's some: Maybe its two thieves at work and you one.

SERVANT. *(terrified)* Ah no, Missus!

MISSUS. Maybe you're joined up with him and looking to get your half evened out to you whilst my back's turned…

SERVANT. *(saying whatever it takes to keep MISSUS from suspecting him)* No, Missus, never! It's all him, as you say! For robbers is everywhere and he's one and it's him robbed you fair and square!

MISSUS. Ah, but I won't be robbed cause I'm rich and don't have to put up with it. *(crafty and cunning)* You hop home and dig out his bag with three coins and run it back whilst I set things up here. For this is my game and nobody beats me at it.

SERVANT. *(only too glad to get out of there)* As you say, Missus.

> *(hurries left and exits)*

MISSUS. *(Going to* MAN. *Pretending great pleasure.)* Here you are at last! I searched the town top to bottom to find you!

MAN. *(holding the bag close and looking uncomfortable)* No need.

> (**SELLERS**, *one by one, notice what is going on and lose interest in their work to watch and listen.)*

MISSUS. Ah, but hear the happy news! Your bag's found! And all three coins safe!

MAN. But this bag and what's in it is mine.

MISSUS. Ah no. My servant got a head full of holes so made a mistake. That's the wrong bag he handed you and here he's coming with yours...

> (**SERVANT** *runs on left with bag of coins)*

And here he is and here it is...

> *(snatches bag from* **SERVANT** *and tries to make* **MAN** *take it)*

And you take yours and I take mine.

> *(attempting to take bag with stones from* **MAN***)*

MAN. *(not letting go)* This bag'll do.

MISSUS. You can't mean it. *(shaking the three coins out of the bag and into her hand)* For here's your own three coins you got a tender feeling for. *(holding the coins out so* MAN *has to look at them)* And see how all three is dented, making them yours for sure?

MAN. *(a careful look at the coins in her hand)* Why, I see they are mine. And I see you know all three's dented, so I suppose you looked in my bag after all.

MISSUS. *(reluctantly)* I suppose I did.

MAN. So I suppose the mistake is yours and not your servant's.

MISSUS. *(more reluctantly)* I suppose it is.

MAN. So I suppose it's your head is full of holes, not his.

MISSUS. *(Has had enough. Shoves bag and coins at* MAN *as she snatches the other bag from him.)* You take yours and give me mine! *(greedily shaking contents of bag into her hand as she walks away)* And here are my… *(stops in her tracks)* Stones? *(looking frantically in bag)* Nothing but stones? *(Rushing back to* MAN. *Furious)* Return my jewels to me at once!

MAN. *(standing his ground)* There's naught to return as they weren't never took. Those stones is your stones, all three. And these coins is my coins, all three.

MISSUS. *(enraged)* Where are my jewels!?

MAN. Home safe and sound and never left. *(looking her in the eye)* But I know when a thief looks at the world, she sees a thief looking back.

MISSUS. *(furious)* Bah!

(Throws the stones. Makes a furious retreat, exiting left with frightened SERVANT *at her heels. All the* SELLERS *roar with laughter.)*

MAN. *(Going to* SELLERS. *Apologetically.)* Rich woman just departed tricked me out of my three coins so I had to trick them back. And I'm sorry for the deception of making use of you in the trick.

FISH SELLER. Here's her fish for your trouble! *(giving fish to* MAN*)*

RICE SELLER. *(giving rice to* MAN*)* Rice to stuff it!

BOTTLE SELLER. *(giving bottle to* MAN*)* This to wash it down!

FLOWER SELLER. *(giving flower to* MAN*)* A flower for your table!

MOUSE SELLER. *(hanging mouse in cage over* MAN's *arm)* And a mouse for luck!

BOTTLE SELLER. And all of it reward!

MAN. *(stunned)* For?

FISH SELLER. For the entertainment of seeing a rich woman puff up…!

FLOWER SELLER. Turn red!

RICE SELLER. And steam off!

    (**SELLERS** *laugh heartily*)

BOTTLE SELLER. *(explaining to* **MAN***)* You see, us who is honest must stick close cause robbers...

ALL. *(***MISSUS** *and* **SERVANT** *come back on. Form line for bow.)* Are everywhere.

    (bow)

COSTUMES

Everyone wears black shirts, black pants, black shoes and
black socks to which they add:

MAN - Ragged tunic and hat

SERVANT - Elegant tunic and hat

MISSUS - Very elegant cape and hat

SELLERS - Simple tunics and hats

SET

Elegant chair left.
5 stools right.

PROPS

3 coins

3 stones the same size and shape as the coins

2 small identical cloth bags

basket of fish

basket of corked bottles

basket of bouquets

basket of rice

basket of small cages with white mice

flashy jewelry

piece of cloth to wrap fish

THE TRIAL OF THE STONE

CHARACTERS

MAN
WOMAN
PRIEST
BAKER
VILLAINS 1 AND 2
SHERIFF
TOWNSPERSONS 1, 2, 3, 4, 5, 6
MALEK
CHILD
GRANDDAD
JUDGE
CLERK

The play is written for a cast of 18. Cast size may be changed by using more or fewer **TOWNSPERSONS**.

Only **MAN** and **WOMAN** are gender specific.

*(Stone at center that is large enough for two people to sit on. It looks heavy but not too heavy to be pried up just a little. **MAN** downstage from stone, holding hat in hand. To audience.)*

MAN. There was a man. Hat on head.

(puts on hat)

Hands in pockets.

(Puts hands in pockets. Takes out one penny.)

One penny from penniless. Alone. When…

(drops penny)

WOMAN. *(Has entered and is strolling by. Picks up penny.)* This yours?

MAN. It is.

WOMAN. *(handing it to him)* Here then.

MAN. *(Takes penny. As they take a few steps away from each other. To audience.)* Did you see her? Like a dream.

WOMAN. *(to audience)* And him? A man among men.

(turning to face each other)

MAN. *(They take a step closer to each other.)* And it's moon…

WOMAN. *(another step closer)* June…

MAN. *(another step closer, extends his hand to her)* Love…

WOMAN. *(another step closer, takes his hand)* Dove…

MAN & WOMAN. *(to audience)* Till next thing you know…

PRIEST. *(Entering. To audience.)* They're calling the priest.

(They arrange themselves for a ceremony. In a ceremonial manner.)

In habitum eternum gravitas. And so married. Done…

PRIEST, MAN AND WOMAN. And done.

*(They clap their hands one quick, hard clap. **PRIEST** exits.)*

MAN. *(happy)* Wife.

WOMAN. *(happy)* Husband.

MAN. *(very serious)* I have bad news.

WOMAN. *(alarmed)* What is it?

MAN. We're poor.

WOMAN. No!

MAN. Yes. But, poor or no, here's my only penny and all I own in the world and so my wedding gift to you. *(gives her penny)*

WOMAN. Husband, this is no ordinary penny. It's the penny found me you and you me. So it's lucky. *(absolutely positive)* And so the cure to our poverty.

MAN. *(doesn't see it)* It's a lowly penny and nothing more and couldn't cure a cold.

WOMAN. Any penny can conjure the miracle of love is lucky and can find us a fortune easy, for fortunes aren't half so rare as love.

MAN. *(willing to be convinced)* I never had me a fortune.

WOMAN. Nor me so we'll have us one together. And we got to go out into the world where fortunes go flying by to give the penny a chance of snagging us one.

MAN. Then the world it is.

(they hold hands and set off walking in a loop around stage)

WOMAN. And they walked themselves away…

MAN. To the end of the day…

MAN & WOMAN. *(walking slower and slower toward stone)* And a terrible… long… walk…

(collapse on to stone)

It was.

MAN. *(weary and discouraged)* Wife, we walked the day start to stop and not a sliver of fortune to show for it.

WOMAN. *(just as weary and discouraged)* Not half a sliver.

MAN. And hungry besides, my insides empty as my pockets.

BAKER. *(enter carrying baskets of bread)* Bread and butter! Butter and bread! Hot from the fire! Two for a penny!

MAN. Ah, the smell makes me swoon!

BAKER. *(hears him and offers two loaves)* Two for a penny, sir!

MAN. *(hopefully)* Wife, the two of us make two. And we got the penny!

WOMAN. Are you mad? It's a lucky penny and not to be spent on the smallness of bread. *(to* **BAKER***)* Nothing for us and on your way.

BAKER. *(shrugs and continues on his way)* Hot buttered bread! Two for a penny! Hot buttered, hot buttered, hot buttered bread!

(exits)

MAN. Wife, our penny had the whole of a day to do the work of raising us a fortune and here we sit sore of foot and starved of stomach and not a fortune in sight.

WOMAN. Don't lucky pennies get tired like all of us? This one here had the strain of searching out us two in all the universe and roping us into the bliss of matrimony and is worn out. It needs resting and after that'll come finding a fortune in the stars and flinging it in our laps.

MAN. *(hand on stomach)* My ears don't hear you so good as my stomach's yelling for bread.

WOMAN. *(hand on stomach)* And mine yelling back. So here's how we spin it. We give the penny one night's rest. Then first thing tomorrow it gets us our fortune. If it don't, I confess the penny lost its luck and ours with it and we use it buying us bread for our breakfast.

MAN. So tomorrow has in it fortune or food?

WOMAN. It has.

MAN. Done and done.

*(***MAN*** and ***WOMAN*** clap hands one quick, hard clap.)*

WOMAN. So we slide it under this stone here.

(They manage to pry up the stone just a little and slide the penny under it.)

WOMAN. *(cont.)* A lucky penny likes the dirt and the dark and is sure to come bouncing out sparkling with luck and that's when you get the most good out of them. And we'll sleep ourselves up close to it.

MAN & WOMAN. Ah, sleeeeep.

(Just saying the word puts them to sleep. They fall asleep sitting on the ground and leaning on the stone. **VILLAINS** 1 *and* 2 *enter, tiptoeing toward stone.)*

VILLAIN 2. *(Stops. Very nervous about all this.)* You dead sure there's a penny?

VILLAIN 1. Have we been dogging them half the day, skulking back of every tree and shrub to keep hid?

VILLAIN 2. We have.

VILLAIN 1. And their voices floating back to us the whole time about their penny they got?

VILLAIN 2. They did.

VILLAIN 1. And me seeing them shove that penny of theirs under that stone they're pillowed up against?

VILLAIN 2. So you say. But I saw nothing.

VILLAIN 1. Cause you're no kind of thief yet, which I am which you won't never be if you don't listen to me. And I say we must expunge the penny from under the stone and into our pockets to buy loathsome frivolities.

VILLAIN 2. *(sympathetically)* Ah, they don't got but a penny. It goes hard to rob them has got so little.

VILLAIN 1. *(not the least bit sympathetic)* They got one penny more than us and that needs reversing. You're not repenting again, are you?

VILLAIN 2. I repent regular but it don't hold. Repenting is slippery.

VILLAIN 1. So not worth the bother. Why, I haven't repented in years and don't miss it. I say, stick to thieving and it'll stick to you. And now to business. We got to get them shook loose of that stone.

(tiptoes to **MAN**, *wiggles hand in front of his face to be sure he's asleep)*

Dreaming.

VILLAIN 2. (**VILLAIN 2** *reluctantly follows* **VILLAIN 1**'s *example. Tiptoes to* **WOMAN** *and wiggles his hand in front of her face.)* Dreaming.

*(***MAN** *and* **WOMAN** *continue sleeping soundly.* **VILLAINS** *nudge* **MAN** *and* **WOMAN** *one, two three times.* **MAN** *and* **WOMAN** *slide a little on each nudge and on the third nudge slowly topple away from stone and continue sleeping on the ground.)*

VILLAIN 1. *(admiring their work)* That's done pretty. Now leverage up the thing.

VILLAIN 2. *(prying up rock with great effort)* I'm leveraging.

VILLAIN 1. *(reaches hand under stone, feeling around)* And... got it!

(He pulls out the penny. **VILLAIN 2** *drops stone and it lands on his foot.)*

VILLAIN 2. Ow!

*(***MAN** *and* **WOMAN** *move around in their sleep)*

VILLAIN 1. Ssshhh! Do you want catching?

(lifts rock with great effort and **VILLAIN 2** *pulls out foot)*

Hoof it!

(they run off)

WOMAN. *(sitting up quickly)* Did you hear that just then? Some sound of rushing away?

MAN. *(sitting up slowly)* All I hear is my poor stomach still singing for bread.

WOMAN. And mine joining the chorus. But don't mind it, for here's morning and now we get out our penny and see if a fortune befalls us. If it don't, we have us hot buttered bread for our breakfast. Give a hand.

(both pushing up stone with great effort)

And...

(**WOMAN** *reaches under stone and searches for penny*)

MAN. And?

WOMAN. *(still searching)* And…

MAN. *(A little impatient. Stone is getting heavier.)* And?

WOMAN. And… *(gives up search)* Gone.

MAN. Gone?!

WOMAN. All dirt and dark and not a penny in it.

MAN. Breadless! *(drops stone)*

WOMAN. Fortuneless!

*(They burst into loud, emotional tears. **SHERIFF** enters, followed by **TOWNSPEOPLE 1, 2** and **3**.)*

SHERIFF. *(to **MAN** and **WOMAN**)* Here now! What's the trouble?

TOWNSPERSON 1. *(yelling to offstage)* There's trouble!

*(**TOWNSPEOPLE 4, 5** and **6** hurry on.)*

SHERIFF. Injured?

TOWNSPERSON 2. *(yelling to offstage)* There's injuries!

*(**MALEK, CHILD** and **GRANDDAD** hurry on.)*

SHERIFF. Lost?

TOWNSPERSON 3. *(yelling to offstage)* All lost!

TOWNSPERSON 4. *(yelling to offstage)* Lost as lambs!

*(**BAKER** and **PRIEST** hurry on. They are all crowding around **MAN** and **WOMAN**, still crying loudly, to get a good look.)*

SHERIFF. *(to crowd with some annoyance)* Stand away! They need quieting!

*(Crowd backs up a little. To **MAN** and **WOMAN** with great authority.)*

I'm sheriff and public displays of despair are illegal in this district!

*(**MAN** and **WOMAN** cry harder. **TOWNSPEOPLE** offer suggestions to **SHERIFF**.)*

TOWNSPERSON 5. Shake pepper on them!

TOWNSPERSON 6. Can't sneeze and cry all at once!

TOWNSPERSON 1. Set their feet in ice!

TOWNSPERSON 2. The shivering will shake the crying straight out of them!

TOWNSPERSON 3. Turn them three turns whilst they whistle!

TOWNSPERSON 4. That'll dizzy them up and air them out and leave them laughing!

*(***JUDGE*** *and* **CLERK** *have entered.* **JUDGE** *carries an elaborately decorated walking stick which he hits one quick, hard hit on floor.)*

CROWD. *(Sees* **JUDGE.** *Very respectfully.)* Your Worship!

JUDGE. *(annoyed)* So here's the hubbub I been hearing.

SHERIFF. It's these two crying and won't leave off.

(a fresh burst of crying from **MAN** *and* **WOMAN**, *louder than ever)*

JUDGE. Is there a cause to the crying?

SHERIFF. I can't get in sideways to ask.

JUDGE. I'll take a swing.

SHERIFF. *(to* **MAN** *and* **WOMAN***)* This here's His Worship and a great personage and so to be heard!

JUDGE. *(to* **MAN** *and* **WOMAN***)* You must cork yourselves or be jailed for stoppage to the public peace.

MAN. *(They manage to stop crying, more or less, and stand to show respect for* **JUDGE.***)* As you say, your worship.

WOMAN. We'll becalm ourselves best we can but know we stand before you robbed.

CROWD. Robbed!

JUDGE. Of?

MAN. Our penny!

TOWNSPERSON 5. Pooh!

TOWNSPERSON 6. A penny's nothing!

TOWNSPERSON 1. A penny's dust!

WOMAN. Robbed of our only penny in the whole of the world.

CROWD. *(instant understanding and sympathy)* Ah.

TOWNSPERSON 2. A heartbreak of villainy!

JUDGE. *(to MAN and WOMAN)* From the start.

WOMAN. Husband and I walked the terrible long walk to here yesterday night, carrying along our lucky penny to land us a fortune.

MAN. We put penny under stone to rest it whilst we had our sleep.

WOMAN. And this morning not a thing under stone but dirt and dark and our penny gone.

JUDGE. So you slid penny under stone. And who saw?

MAN. Not a soul but ourselves.

JUDGE. So there was naught but you and you and the stone here when you secreted your penny away beneath it?

WOMAN. True as trout.

JUDGE. Sheriff!

SHERIFF. Your Worship?

JUDGE. Arrest the stone!

SHERIFF. *(confused)* The stone, sire?

JUDGE. The stone! For it is the stone stole their penny!

SHERIFF. Stone, you are arrested in the name of the commonwealth! For robbery to a penny!

JUDGE. And to be hauled to court forthwith!

SHERIFF. *(to the crowd)* You heard him, boys! All grab hold.

(several **TOWNSPEOPLE** *crowd around the stone)*

And lift!

(They try to lift the stone. It doesn't budge.)

Stone won't be lifted, sire.

JUDGE. So court to be hauled here forthwith and on your toes!

*(***ALL*** *go off and bring on stools.* **JUDGE,** *with tallest stool, stands behind stone. Others arrange themselves left*

and right of stone, holding stools. As they are doing this,
VILLAINS *sneak on carrying stools.* **VILLAIN 2** *changes
his mind and starts to exit.)*

VILLAIN 1. *(stopping* **VILLAIN 2***)* What you doing hanging
back? Here's a crowd of pockets need picking and us
the men for the job.

VILLAIN 2. This is maybe not so bright, our recent crime
being the cause of the commotion.

VILLAIN 1. Are we villains or are we not?

VILLAIN 2. *(not at all sure)* We are?

VILLAIN 1. We are! And as villains we got to do our duty
and steal them blind whilst we can. Plus, we got a mob
arresting a stone so not a brain amongst them. We'll
slick this crowd easy. *(drags* **VILLAIN 2** *along with him and
they blend into the crowd)*

CLERK. Done and done!

*(***JUDGE** *hits stick one quick, hard hit on floor and* **ALL**
clap hands one quick, hard clap. Sit on stools.)

Order in the court! His Honor and Worship presiding!

JUDGE. Clerk, inflict the oath.

CLERK. *(stands, faces stone and raises a hand)* Swear to speak
the truth or be flummoxed. *(Waits for stone's reply. To*
JUDGE.*)* Your Worship, accused don't raise a hand so
besmirches the oath.

JUDGE. *(to stone)* You stand unoathed but if you lie we'll
ferret it out and flummoxing will follow.
Name?

(waits for stone's reply)

Speak up bright and clear so all can hear!

(waits for stone's reply)

Not speaking at court is an old trick been done before
so don't work. Court names accused "Stone." Done
and done.

(One quick, hard hit of the stick on the floor and **ALL**
clap hands one quick, hard clap.)

Residence?

(Waits again. With some impatience)

Where do you live, Stone?

MALEK. *(standing)* A word, sire?

JUDGE. Will there be benefit to trial?

MALEK. That is my hope.

JUDGE. *(to* **CLERK***)* Oath 'em.

MALEK. **(CLERK** *goes to* **MALEK** *and both raise a hand)* If I speak ought but truth, may my toes turn to snakes whilst I sleep.

   *(***JUDGE** *hits stick one quick, hard hit on floor and* **ALL** *clap one quick, hard clap.* **VILLAIN** 1 *steals a scarf from* **TOWNSPERSON** 1 *in such a way that the audience sees him do it. No one on stage notices.)*

JUDGE. *(to* **MALEK***)* From the start.

MALEK. I walk this road to and from my field, so every day twice, and that stone is here in every instance and no variety. So I suppose this is its place it lives.

JUDGE. Do you give a name to this place?

MALEK. Half the walk to Malek's field, I suppose, me being Malek. *(sits)*

JUDGE. Stone's place it lives is Half The Walk To Malek's Field. Done and done.

   (hits the stick one quick, hard hit on floor and **ALL** *clap hands one quick, hard clap. To stone.)*

Age?

(Waits again. Trying to be reasonable.)

Come now, Stone. Unbend some, can't you?

CHILD. *(stands up)* Beg pardon, sire?

JUDGE. Yes, child?

CHILD. The old granddad has some to say.

JUDGE. *(to* **CLERK***)* Get 'em oathed.

CHILD. **(CLERK** *goes to* **CHILD** *and* **GRANDDAD**. *They all raise a hand.)* What we say is here true or may we suffer seven years bewretchment of boils and bats.

(*JUDGE hits stick one quick, hard hit on floor and* **ALL** *clap one quick, hard clap.* **VILLAIN 2** *steals onions from* **TOWNSPERSON 2** *in such a way that the audience sees it. No one on stage notices.*)

JUDGE. *(to* **CHILD***)* Speak up, child.

CHILD. The old granddad here says stone is known to him his whole life from boy to today.

JUDGE. And how old is the old granddad?

CHILD. (**GRANDAD** *whispers in her ear. To* **JUDGE***.*) 93…

(**GRANDAD** *whispers again*)

And three quarters…

(**GRANDAD** *whispers again*)

Last July…

(**GRANDAD** *whispers again*)

The 12th.

JUDGE. Court assigns stone the age of 93 and three quarters.

(**GRANDAD** *whispers to* **CHILD** *again*)

What's he say, child?

CHILD. Old enough to know better.

(*JUDGE hits stick one quick, hard hit on floor and* **ALL** *clap one quick, hard clap.* **CHILD** *sits.*)

JUDGE. Stone, when last was you in trouble with the law? (*Waits again. Out of patience with it.*) As you won't say, I ask the crowd here present: Do any know Stone to be careless of the law?

(*murmuring among the crowd*)

BAKER. *(stands)* We say Stone's innocent of all crime till today…

MALEK. *(stands)* So far as we know…

PRIEST. *(stands)* So help us heaven.

(*JUDGE hits stick one quick, hard hit on floor and* **ALL** *clap one quick, hard clap.* **BAKER**, **MALEK** *and* **PRIEST** *sit.*)

JUDGE. And so to the crime at hand. Are victims here present?

WOMAN. Here, Your Worship.

*(**MAN** and **WOMAN** stand)*

JUDGE. Oath 'em up.

MAN. *(**CLERK** goes to **MAN** and **WOMAN**. All three raise a hand.)* If we lie here in the sancity of the court, may dragons come flying out our ears and set up house in our hair...

WOMAN. And go to stinking and smoking and roaring and eating pickles all over the place up there.

*(**JUDGE** hits stick one quick, hard hit on floor and **ALL** clap one quick, hard clap. **VILLAIN** 1 steals a feather off of **TOWNSPERSON** 3's hat and **VILLAIN** 2 steals a string of sundries from **TOWNSPERSON** 4 in such a way that audience sees it. No one on stage notices.)*

JUDGE. *(to **MAN** and **WOMAN**)* When first you came upon Stone, what did Stone say?

WOMAN. Not a word.

JUDGE. As you spoke amongst yourselves, did Stone listen?

MAN. Well, it was right there beneath us as we sat upon it and we wasn't whispering.

JUDGE. And did you see Stone to behave suspiciously at all?

WOMAN. I never saw Stone to act any way, as is mostly how it goes with stones.

JUDGE. Have you aught to add?

MAN. Only that we done not one thing to Stone to precipitate the revenge of robbery.

*(**MAN** and **WOMAN** sit.)*

JUDGE. And now to the stone. *(trying to be fair)* Stone, this here's your first crime ever you done so we'll be kind if we can. But you got to confess it or say it isn't so. How say you as regards said penny? *(waits again)* Stone, speak now or wish you had for we mean business and you could land in lock-up which is a generally unclean and upsetting place. *(as though Stone has spoken)* Eh? *(leans in to stone and listens intently)* Ah. *(with great interest)* Really?

CLERK. Is Stone confessing, Your Worship?

JUDGE. No. *(as he scans the crowd with a hard, accusing look)* Stone is… accusing!

VILLAIN 2. *(coming forward with great emotion)* That stone's a liar! I didn't steal that penny nor nothing! And neither did my partner there! *(pointing to **VILLAIN 1**)*

JUDGE. Didn't you?

VILLAIN 2. No sir! Plus you can't prove it for we spent the penny!

JUDGE. On what?

VILLAIN 2. Cigars and a gristle of meat!

VILLAIN 1. *(has managed to get his hand over **VILLAIN 2**'s mouth)* Shut it! *(to **JUDGE**)* We got no penny no where on us. And without a penny there's no proof and we walk away free. *(trying to leave and dragging **VILLAIN 2** with him)*

TOWNSPERSON 1. *(Sees scarf in **VILLAIN 1**'s pocket. Pulls it out.)* My comfrey!

TOWNSPERSON 2. *(Sees onions in **VILLAIN 2**'s pocket. Pulls them out.)* My hoohaws!

TOWNSPERSON 3. *(pulls feather from **VILLAIN 1**'s pocket)* My mum's fergus!

TOWNSPERSON 4. *(pulls assorted sundries from **VILLAIN 2**'s pocket)* My assorted sundries!

JUDGE. No penny for proof you say, but this'll do. The commonwealth charges you with committing grand larceny upon the comfrey, the hoohaw, his mum's fergus and the assorted sundries. You ought to be ashamed. Haul them to lock-up, Sheriff.

SHERIFF. Yes, Your Worship!

*(grabs **VILLAINS** and is hauling them off)*

VILLAIN 1. *(To **VILLAIN 2**. Profoundly discouraged.)* Ah, you got us grabbed.

VILLAIN 2. I smelt ourselves caught so lied hard as I could.

VILLAIN 1. Your lying stinks bad as your thieving.

    (**SHERIFF** *and* **VILLAINS** *exit*)

TOWNSPERSON 3. Show over!

TOWNSPERSON 4. Back to the hives!

    (**TOWNSPEOPLE** *get up to leave*)

JUDGE. *(very in charge)* Sit!

    (**TOWNSPEOPLE** *sit reluctantly*)

Court don't end till I end it. I judge all here guilty.

TOWNSPERSON 5. *(indignant)* Us?

TOWNSPERSON 6. *(more indignant)* Of?

JUDGE. Of thinking a stone to be a thief!

BAKER. *(most indignant)* Why, it was you got us started!

JUDGE. Nothing draws a thief like a crowd and nothing draws a crowd like a trial. And I know a thief is fast to yell out his innocence every chance he gets. An honest man don't bother. So I arrested the stone to make a trial to pull in a crowd to pull in the thieves and in they came and there they are in lock-up. I'm not a judge by accident but know the trade.

WOMAN. *(to* **MAN***)* A judge among judges.

JUDGE. I am that. And all the rest ought to know better! A stone stealing pennies! And next it'll be shoes robbing banks, I suppose? Or chairs stealing chickens? I fine each one here a penny apiece for the crime of no sense. Clerk'll pass the hat…

(Takes off his hat and hands it to **CLERK** *who passes it around.* **ALL** *begrudgingly drop in pennies.)*

Whilst I denounce my perjuries to the stone which is as innocent and moral and decent a stone as ever was.

MAN. *(to* **WOMAN***)* A stone among stones.

WOMAN. (**WOMAN** *and* **MAN** *stand and get ready to leave*) And we'll blow back the way we come.

JUDGE. Not so fast for here's the collection . . .

*(He gestures for the **CLERK** to hand them the hat which has completed its rounds.)*

And all of it yours as remedy for being robbed and to show we here aren't all villains and thieves.

CLERK. *(presenting the hat full of pennies)* A pound of pennies.

MAN. *(taking the hat and looking into it in disbelief)* A fortune!

WOMAN. I grieve the loss of our lucky penny but I see now how it done its work and got us our fortune we longed for.

MAN. And here it is!

WOMAN. And here we are in this blessed corner of the world where we was handed a fortune and it ought to be home.

MAN. And home it is. *(gesturing right of stone)* Here a house.

WOMAN. *(gesturing left of stone)* Here a garden.

MAN. *(sitting on stone)* And here our stone.

WOMAN. *(sitting on stone)* Our lucky stone!

MAN AND WOMAN. Done…

*(**ALL** form line on either side of them. **SHERIFF** and **VILLAINS** come out to join line.)*

ALL. And done!

*(**JUDGE** hits floor one quick, hard hit with stick and **ALL** clap hands one quick, hard clap. Bow heads.)*

COSTUMES

All wear plain black pants, shirts, shoes and socks to which is added:

MAN - Plain tunic and hat

WOMAN - Plain skirt. Plain scarves tied over hair and around waist.

PRIEST - Black cape and clerical hat

BAKER - White baker's apron and hat

VILLAINS - Nasty black tunics with pockets. Nasty black hats.

SHERIFF and **CLERK** - Fancy tunics and hats befitting their offices.

TOWNSPEOPLE, MALEK, CHILD and **GRANDDAD** - Men wear simple, colorful tunics and hats. Women wear simple, colorful skirts and have colorful scarves tied over hair and around waists.

JUDGE - Elaborate black robe and hat befitting his high station.

SET

A large stone

18 stools. **JUDGE**'s stool is taller than the others.

PROPS

15 pennies

Basket with loaves of bread

Elaborately decorated walking stick.

A long brightly colored scarf (comfrey)

String of onions (hoohaws)

Hat with a big feather (fergus)

A variety of odd objects tied together with ribbons (assorted sundries)

Also by
Colleen Neuman...

Lion and Mouse Stories

The Princess Plays

THREEE: Three Funny Folktales

Please visit our website **bakersplays.com** for complete
descriptions and licensing information.

www.ingramcontent.com/pod-product-compliance
Lightning Source LLC
Chambersburg PA
CBHW050627070726
47592CB00028B/1708